WHY IS THE SKY BLUE?

by Debbie Vilardi

Cody Koala

An Imprint of Pop!
popbooksonline.com

abdobooks.com
Published by Pop!, a division of ABDO, PO Box 398166, Minneapolis, Minnesota 55439. Copyright © 2019 by POP, LLC. International copyrights reserved in all countries. No part of this book may be reproduced in any form without written permission from the publisher. Pop!™ is a trademark and logo of POP, LLC.

Printed in the United States of America, North Mankato, Minnesota
092018
012019
THIS BOOK CONTAINS RECYCLED MATERIALS

Cover Photo: iStockphoto
Interior Photos: iStockphoto, 1, 6, 15, 19 (bottom left), 20–21; Shutterstock Images, 5, 9, 10, 19 (top), 19 (bottom right); Red Line Editorial, 13; Johnson Space Center/NASA, 16

Editor: Meg Gaertner
Series Designer: Laura Mitchell

Library of Congress Control Number: 2018950147
Publisher's Cataloging-in-Publication Data
Names: Vilardi, Debbie, author.
Title: Why is the sky blue? / by Debbie Vilardi.
Description: Minneapolis, Minnesota : Pop!, 2019 | Series: Science questions | Includes online resources and index.
Identifiers: ISBN 9781532162206 (lib. bdg.) | ISBN 9781641855914 (pbk) | ISBN 9781532163265 (ebook)
Subjects: LCSH: Sky--Juvenile literature. | Sky--Color--Juvenile literature. | Color in nature--Juvenile literature. | Children's questions and answers--Juvenile literature.
Classification: DDC 500--dc23

Hello! My name is
Cody Koala

Pop open this book and you'll find QR codes like this one, loaded with information, so you can learn even more!

Scan this code* and others like it while you read, or visit the website below to make this book pop.

popbooksonline.com/sky-blue

*Scanning QR codes requires a web-enabled smart device with a QR code reader app and a camera.

Table of Contents

Chapter 1
Atmosphere 4

Chapter 2
Sunlight 8

Chapter 3
Scattered Light 14

Chapter 4
Sight 18

Making Connections 22
Glossary 23
Index 24
Online Resources 24

Chapter 1

Atmosphere

A thick layer of air surrounds Earth. This air is Earth's **atmosphere**. People cannot see it. But it is filled with many tiny air **particles**.

> The atmosphere can be seen from space.

Watch a video here!

6

Sunlight passes through the atmosphere. It hits the air particles. The light **scatters**. It makes the sky appear blue.

Chapter 2

Sunlight

Sunlight appears to be white. But it contains all colors. The colors separate when sunlight passes through a **prism**. Colors separate by their **wavelengths**.

Learn more here!

high point

low point

Think of ocean waves. Each wave has a high point and a low point. A wavelength is the distance between two high points or two low points.

Each color has a different wavelength. The wavelength for blue light is short. The wavelength for red light is long.

> Raindrops can act like prisms. Sunlight hits them. A rainbow appears.

Wavelengths

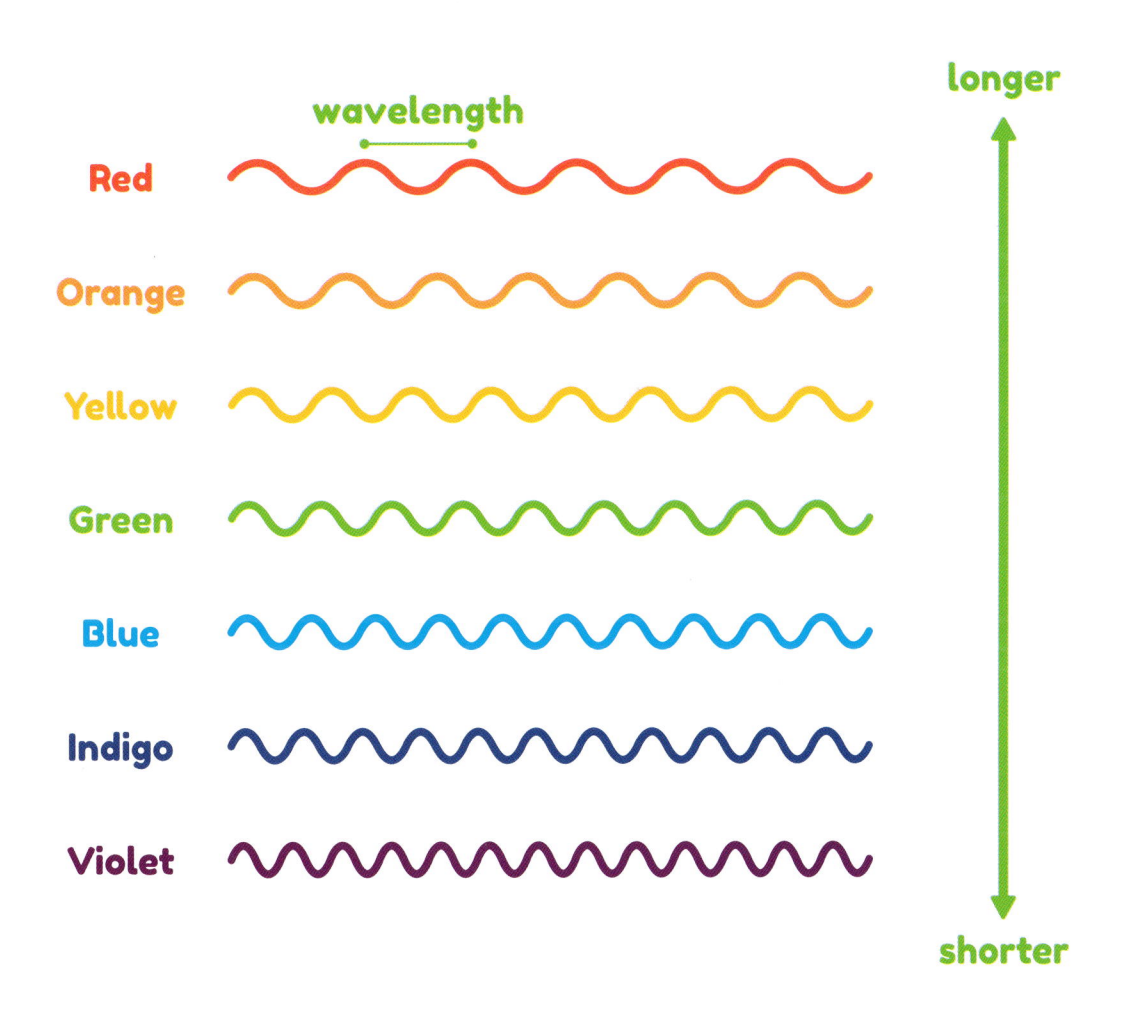

wavelength

Red

Orange

Yellow

Green

Blue

Indigo

Violet

longer

shorter

Chapter 3

Scattered Light

Sunlight enters the atmosphere. It makes air particles move up and down. This movement scatters the light in all directions. Each color scatters differently.

Learn more here!

15

16

Blue light makes the particles move fast. They scatter more light. Red light does not move the particles as much. People see more blue than red in the sky.

> The moon has a thin atmosphere. Its sky is fully dark at night. During the day it is covered in white sunlight.

Chapter 4

Sight

Violet light has a shorter wavelength than blue light. It scatters even more light. But human eyes are more **sensitive** to blue light. They see a blue sky.

Complete an activity here!

19

Sunsets are not blue. The sun is low on the **horizon**. Sunlight has to travel through more of the atmosphere.

Blue light scatters before it reaches people's eyes. Reds and yellows are left.

Making Connections

Text-to-Self

Have you seen a sunset or sunrise? What colors did you see?

Text-to-Text

Have you read other books about the sky or the atmosphere? What new thing did you learn?

Text-to-World

Light travels in waves. What else travels in waves?

Glossary

atmosphere – the layer of gases that surrounds a planet.

horizon – the line at which the sky appears to touch the Earth's surface.

particle – a tiny piece of something.

prism – a glass object that bends light and separates it into colors.

scatter – to separate in all directions.

sensitive – quick to see or react to something.

wavelength – the distance from the highest point of one wave to the highest point of the next.

Index

atmosphere, 4, 7, 14, 17, 20

colors, 8, 12, 14

light, 7, 8, 12, 14, 17, 18, 20–21

particles, 4, 7, 14, 17

prism, 8, 12

sunsets, 20

wavelengths, 8, 11–13, 18

Online Resources

popbooksonline.com

Thanks for reading this Cody Koala book!

Scan this code* and others like it in this book, or visit the website below to make this book pop!

popbooksonline.com/sky-blue

*Scanning QR codes requires a web-enabled smart device with a QR code reader app and a camera.